by **Margery Cuyler**

illustrated by **Arthur Howard**

BULLIES NEVER WIN

Simon & Schuster Books for Young Readers

New York   London   Toronto   Sydney

For Sarah and Don Thomas, who are anything but bullies—M. C.

SIMON & SCHUSTER BOOKS FOR YOUNG READERS
An imprint of Simon & Schuster Children's Publishing Division
1230 Avenue of the Americas, New York, New York 10020
Text copyright © 2009 by Margery Cuyler
Illustrations copyright © 2009 by Arthur Howard
SIMON & SCHUSTER BOOKS FOR YOUNG READERS is a trademark of
Simon & Schuster, Inc.
Book design by Laurent Linn
The text for this book is set in Adobe Garamond.
The illustrations for this book are rendered in pen and ink with watercolor paints.
Manufactured in China
2 4 6 8 10 9 7 5 3 1
Library of Congress Cataloging-in-Publication Data
Cuyler, Margery.
Bullies never win / Margery Cuyler ; illustrated by Arthur Howard.—1st ed.
p. cm.
Summary: First-grader Jessica worries about everything Brenda the bully
might tease her about, until the day she has had enough and discovers a new way to deal with Brenda.
ISBN: 978-0-689-86187-1 (hardcover)
[1. Bullies—Fiction. 2. Worry—Fiction. 3. Teasing—Fiction. 4. Self-perception—Fiction. 5. Friendship—Fiction.]
I. Howard, Arthur, ill. II. Title.
PZ7.C997Br 2009
[E]—dc22
2007045251

Jessica was a worrier.
She worried night and day.

She worried about her socks
not matching

and having knobby knees

and losing her barrettes

and not doing well in school.

But in Mr. Martin's first-grade class,
Jessica had a *big* worry: Brenda Bailey.

Brenda was perfect.
Her bangs were even.
Her homework was always right.

She wore a new outfit every day,

and she scowled when Jessica
did something better than she did.

If Jessica got all her
homework right, Brenda
would say, "I bet you cheated."
So Jessica hid her homework.

If Jessica wore a new skirt to school, Brenda
would say, "Your legs look like toothpicks."
So Jessica started wearing pants.

If Jessica scored at kickball, Brenda
would say, "You were just lucky."
So Jessica stopped playing kickball.

Brenda never asked Jessica to sit with her at lunch. Instead Brenda sat with all her friends and Jessica sat alone.

Jessica got tired of sitting by herself, so one day she tried sitting at Brenda's table.

"Look who's here. Toothpick!"

Jessica's eyes started to sting. She blinked to keep from crying. She left the cafeteria without finishing her lunch.

After school Jessica went to her room. She stared at the wall. She worried.

What terrible thing would Brenda say next? Jessica thought about Mr. Martin. He had told the class that sometimes bullies stop bullying if you just ignore them.

But how could Jessica ignore a bully who was always in her face?

At dinner Dad asked, "How was school?"
Jessica stared at her food.
"What's wrong?" asked Mom.
"Nothing," said Jessica.

That night Jessica couldn't fall asleep. She squeezed her eyes shut and tried to count sheep, but instead she saw perfect little Brendas leaping over the fence.

The next morning her eyes felt as dry as sand and her stomach hurt.

"Can I stay home today?" she asked Mom.
Her mother felt her forehead. "You don't feel hot."
"I have a stomachache," said Jessica.
"I guess you *are* sick," said Mom. "Go back to bed."
Immediately Jessica's stomach felt better.

But she knew she couldn't avoid Brenda forever.
So the following day Jessica went to school.

All morning Jessica ignored Brenda. But
at lunchtime she discovered that Mom had
packed her sandwich in Tom's lunch box.

She tried to shove it behind her back
before Brenda could see.

But she wasn't quick enough.

"Toothpick has a *boy's* lunch box,"
Brenda said to everyone.

Jessica's cheeks felt like chili peppers.
How could Mom have made such a mistake?

"Come sit over here," called Anita.
Jessica quickly sat down next to Anita and her friends.
"That Brenda's such a bully!" said Anita. "You should stand up to her."
But Jessica couldn't.

When she got home, Jessica told her mother, "You packed my lunch in *Tom's* lunch box. It's a *boy's* lunch box."

"I was in a hurry," said Mom. "I'm sorry." She paused. "What difference does it make? Your lunch is your lunch, no matter what it's packed in."

"It makes a BIG difference," said Jessica,
and she burst into tears.

"This can't be just about lunch boxes," said Mom.

"It's about Brenda," said Jessica, hiccupping between sobs. "She picks on me. She calls me Toothpick. Today she teased me about Tom's lunch box."

"That's terrible," said Mom. "Have you told her how you feel?"

"No," cried Jessica. "Then she'd *really* make fun of me."

"Why don't you talk to Mr. Martin?" suggested Mom. "If he knew that Brenda was bullying you, he'd do something about it."

That night Jessica tossed and turned. Should she talk to Mr. Martin? Should she stand up to Brenda?

What could she say to her? Your bangs are ugly? Your knees are flat as pancakes? Your freckles look like pimples?

The next morning Brenda came up behind Jessica in the hallway.

"Toothpick!" Brenda hissed.

Jessica's heart began to pound. She thought about what her mother had said. She turned around and blurted, "I'm going to tell Mr. Martin if you keep picking on me!"

"Tattletale," said Brenda, and she stuck out her tongue and ran into the classroom.

At lunch Jessica sat with Anita again.

Brenda was at the next table with all her friends. "Hey, Toothpick!" called Brenda. "Did you bring your brother's lunch box again? No wonder you're so skinny. You eat baby food."

Jessica stood up. Enough was enough!
She put her hands on her hips. In a loud voice she said, "Toothpicks may be thin, but bullies never win!"

Brenda blushed. Her freckles
turned pink.
For once, she didn't say anything.

Jessica threw back her shoulders
and marched out of the cafeteria.

At dinner Laura asked, "Did you stand up to that bully Brenda?"

"Why didn't she like my lunch box?" asked Tom.

"Pass the spaghetti," said Dad.

"How'd things go?" asked Mom.

"I don't think Brenda will pick on me anymore," said Jessica. "But even if she does, I know what to do."

"Hooray for Jessica!" said her family.

"Hooray for toothpicks!" said Jessica.

And that night Jessica fell asleep
without any more worries.